SCOOTER SPIES

THE WHEELS THAT VANISHED

MICHAEL DAHL

A MINSTREL® BOOK

Published by POCKET BOOKS

New York   London   Toronto   Sydney   Singapore

A MINSTREL PAPERBACK *Original*

A Minstrel Book published by
POCKET BOOKS, a division of Simon & Schuster, Inc.
1230 Avenue of the Americas, New York, NY 10020

Copyright © 2000 by Michael Dahl

ISBN: 0-7434-1877-8

First Minstrel Books printing December 2000

10 9 8 7 6 5 4 3 2

A MINSTREL BOOK and colophon are registered trademarks of Simon & Schuster, Inc.

Cover art by Don Stewart

Printed in the U.S.A.

To Danny Thomas
who walked across the Mixaloopi River bridge

1

THE WHEELS
THAT VANISHED

BONG . . . BONG . . .

The hundred-year-old clock tower that stood at the center of the University of Metroville boomed out the hour.

Eleven-year-old Max Martin looked down at the small clock attached to the handlebars of his scooter. Two o'clock. His dad would be finished teaching his astronomy class in fifteen minutes at the Space Science Center. In less than twenty minutes, Max would meet his dad at the parking lot in front of the Center.

Max loved riding his scooter through the backstreets of the University. He glanced around at a dim alley he was gliding through. *This must be near the Biology Building.* Max followed a narrow passage as it angled between smooth concrete walls.

Dylan's motorcycle would never fit through here, Max thought with a grin. *I'll have to tell him at dinner.* Max and his older brother Dylan were always arguing about which was the better set of wheels: motorcycle or scooter. Max kept a growing list of advantages for scooters beginning with:

#1. Athletes ride scooters.

"You need strong legs to ride a scooter," Max told his brother over dinner last night. "And good reflexes and—"

"In other words, you should be like me," said Dylan.

"If you're so good, why don't you run to soccer practice next time instead of riding your stupid motorcycle?" Max asked.

"Stupid? My bike can circle the U. ten times before your scooter makes it around once."

"Big deal," said Max. "At least I'm not wasting gas."

"Cycles get excellent mileage," said Dylan. "I'd still have plenty of gas."

"You have plenty of gas all right," laughed Max.

"All right, all right," said Mr. Martin at the head of the dinner table. "That's the last time I serve Seven Bean Casserole."

As he kicked his scooter through the alley, Max added another item to his list.

#2. Scooters can ride through the Biology Building alley without scraping the walls.

Up ahead, another scooter in the alley was aiming straight toward him.

Max braced both feet on the aluminum deck. *This alley is too narrow. That kid is gonna crash right into me.*

He gripped the handlebars and felt the rush of wind as the other scooter rocketed past. Something cool on the other scooter's deck brushed against his feet. At the end of the alley he skidded to a stop and looked behind him. The other kid had also stopped. Max gave him a thumbs-up.

"Smooth ride," said the other kid.

A flash of neon green snagged Max's attention. Something whizzed past him in the small courtyard behind the Bio Building.

The green blur vanished behind the side of the building. By the time Max reached the corner of the building, the blur had disappeared. Was it a bike?

Max rode back through the alley. He saw nothing in front or in back of the building. The neon- green blur had simply vanished. And so had the other scooter. *Maybe the blur zipped inside the Bio Building,* thought Max. *No, the doors are locked since most classes ended yesterday.* Max's dad was teaching an extra session today to help students who had been out with an early winter flu.

Max and his silver scooter made a large circuit around the Bio Building. He glided through courtyards, bumped across cobblestone paths, and snaked between stone benches until he returned to the mouth of the same alley where he had rocketed past the kid on the red scooter. *There it was again!* Fifty yards away, zipping beneath a line of palm trees, raced the strangest bicycle Max had ever seen.

The bike was neon green. It had red spokeless wheels and seemed to be made out of wires instead of aluminum tubing. The reddish wheels reminded Max of the wheels on a kid's wagon or on a wheelbarrow. The bike disappeared behind a hedge of bushes and palm trees that lined the sidewalk in front of the Biology Building.

"Stop that bike!" yelled a voice.

A woman wearing a long skirt and a pink blouse ran up to Max. She was breathing hard. Max recognized her as one of the University's teachers.

She pointed toward the bushes and yelled, "That thief stole my—"

Max didn't stay to hear her finish the sentence. He kicked off and steered his scooter to follow the bike's trail.

On the other side of the bushes and palms, Max

spied the strange bike heading toward the River Bridge. The University of Metroville was built on both sides of the wide Mixaloopi River. The Mixaloopi emptied into the Gulf of Mexico less than a mile away. A tall bridge connected the two banks. The bridge had two levels. The lower level was an asphalt-covered road for cars and trucks. The upper level had a covered walkway running down its middle that students used when it rained in winter or was too hot in summer. Max saw the neon-green bike zoom up the ramp to the walkway and zip inside. It was too far away for Max to catch up with it.

"Where'd it go?" yelled a new voice. Max turned and saw a young, skinny University security guard trotting toward him. At his side jogged the teacher.

"Where'd it go?" repeated the guard.

"On the bridge," Max pointed. "In the walk-way."

"What were you doing in the alley?" asked the guard. He frowned at Max.

"Riding," said Max.

The skinny security guard spoke sharply into his two-way radio. He alerted guards at the other end of the bridge. "The suspect should be exiting the walkway on the west side in about a minute." Then the guard turned his attention back to Max.

"What did he look like?"

"He?" asked Max.

"The rider of the so-called bicycle," said the guard.

He? Was the thief a he or she? Max tried to remember. "I'm not sure," answered Max.

The guard gave Max a funny look.

The radio sputtered loudly in the guard's fist. "Where is he? Over."

The guard held the radio to his mouth. "He must be at your end by now. We saw him enter the walkway thirty seconds ago. Over."

Wrong, thought Max, I *saw him enter the walkway thirty seconds ago.*

There was a pause from the radio.

Max, the guard, and the teacher walked up the ramp to the walkway. "I don't see him," the guard said. The bridge was a quarter-mile long. Max spied a few figures walking at the other end. Not a single bike in sight.

"I need to get back to the Bio Lab," said the teacher. She hurried back down the ramp.

The radio squawked again. "No bikes here. Over."

"You couldn't miss it," said the skinny guard.

"I'm not blind," said the radio. "Walk over here yourself, bud."

The security guard squinted at Max. "You sure you saw that bike go in here?"

"Yeah. It raced inside and headed over the river."

"Maybe not," said the guard. "Maybe, after you

turned around, it doubled back and came out this side."

There wasn't enough time, thought Max. He noticed a teenage girl reading on a cement bench near the entrance to the walkway. A big canvas backpack was squeezed under the seat. "Ask her," said Max.

The guard walked over, hands on hips, and questioned the girl. She replied that she had seen the strange-looking bike rush past her into the walkway. "But I didn't see it come out," she said. "I'm sure I would have remembered. It was such an odd contraption."

"Think you could identify the rider?" asked the guard.

"I'm sorry, I didn't get a good look. It was so fast."

The radio squawked. "Repeat: Where is the bike? Over."

The guard sighed. "I'm walking over to your side," he replied into the radio.

Max followed the guard inside the walkway. It was deserted except for two students, a boy and a girl. They were strolling over from the far west bank. The guard halted and questioned them.

"Yeah, we saw it," said the boy, running a hand through his bright pink hair. A gold stud glittered on the left side of his nose. "It was way weird."

"It didn't look like a normal bike," said the girl.

She had short, inky-black hair and wore army pants. "The wheels were funny looking."

"They were orange," said the boy.

"Red," corrected the girl. "And they didn't have spokes."

"Did you notice the rider?" asked the guard.

The boy and girl stared at each other. "It was just a regular guy," said the boy.

"It was a girl," said the girl.

"It was a guy," said the boy. "And he was wearing combat boots."

"*She* was wearing black athletic shoes."

Max smiled to himself. They hadn't gotten a good look at the rider either. Their attention had been glued to the bike itself, just as Max's had been.

"Did you see anyone else?" asked the guard.

"Nope," said the girl. "And you can't miss anyone inside here."

That was true, thought Max. The walkway was about twenty feet wide, the length of two police cars. Perfect for scooter races. Windows ran along both sides. A high ceiling held fluorescent lights for walking at night. Max saw square white panels next to some of the lights. The panels were entrances to the walkway's roof. *Were they big enough for a bike to squeeze through?* he wondered. The roof looked strong enough to support a bike and rider.

Max added to his list:

 # 3. Scooters are light enough for roofs. Motorcycles are not.

"When the bike passed you, didn't you turn around and watch it?" asked the guard. "Weren't you curious?"

"Maybe for a sec," said the boy. "Then we kept walking."

"I've got a bus to catch on the east side of the river," said the girl.

Max glanced over at the west end of the walkway. Over a hundred feet away, the other security guards were gathered outside the walkway doors. Somewhere in that hundred feet of empty space, between the guards and where Max now stood, a bike and rider had vanished.

"See or hear anything unusual?" asked the guard.

The boy and girl both shook their heads. The boy shrugged off the backpack he was carrying and pulled out a plastic container of water. He squirted some in his mouth. "I heard something like squealing tires below us, but that was all."

Max could feel the vibration of the traffic rumbling beneath his scooter's wheels.

"Squealing tires, huh?" asked the guard.

The boy student nodded.

"Car tires or truck tires?"

"How can you tell the difference?" asked the boy.

"I didn't hear anything," said the inky-haired girl.

Max glanced out one of the walkway's windows. The surface of the Mixaloopi River was seventy feet below them. Was it possible for a person on the bridge to hear a splash in the river?

"Can I go now, please?" pleaded the girl. "I don't want to miss my bus."

The guard slowly pulled a notepad out of his shirt pocket and recorded the students' names. He wrote Max's name, too.

"You live around here, kid?" asked the guard.

"My dad is Robert Martin and he teaches in the Space Science Center," said Max. His dad! He had forgotten all about him. The clock on his scooter read 2:25.

Max jumped onto the solid aluminum deck of his scooter and pushed against the concrete floor of the walkway with a sneakered toe. Soon he was zinging away in a silver flash toward the eastern end of the bridge. The skinny guard and the two students were specks in his rearview mirror. Max gripped the handlebars and prayed that his dad was still waiting for him in the parking lot out front of the Center.

Wait 'til he heard about the vanishing bike!

2

ICE BOY

"Oscar! *¡Date prisa!* Hurry! Two bags of ice to the Riverside Dorm."

Oscar Santiago stacked the two blue plastic bags his father handed him one at a time. He bungee-corded the bags on the back of his long-tailed scooter in one swift, sure move. "Riverside again?" he asked.

His father nodded. "Six dollars. Room 214. Think you can do it under ten minutes?"

Oscar grinned. "Under seven, Papi."

The scooter gleamed like a ruby in the afternoon sun. Oscar kicked away from the back of his father's grocery store and headed to the University of Metroville.

"Careful!" yelled his father in the distance. "There's construction."

Oscar reached the entrance to the University in less than a minute. He zoomed past the ancient stone gates. He flew in between strolling students, rushing teachers, bikers, boarders, and other scooters on their way to vacations and parties. Winter break was Oscar's favorite time for running deliveries. Everyone needed extra ice for their parties and picnics, and his father's grocery store was the closest supply of ice for the entire University. Oscar and his well-worn wheels kept busy morning to late afternoon whisking bags of frozen blue ice all over campus.

ROOBICK'S CUBES said the blue plastic. Oscar knew that Roobick's was the best tasting ice in the country. Even soda pop that had lost its fizz tasted better once the blue-tinted ice cubes were plopped into a glass.

Oscar enjoyed seeing the surprised expression on his customers' faces when he knocked on their doors. "Wow! That was fast!" they always exclaimed. When they noticed Oscar's scooter, they always added, "Where's the motor on that thing?" An elderly University professor once told Oscar that he must have legs of steel to make such quick deliveries. Some of the students nicknamed Oscar Ice Boy.

"Because I'm so cool," he joked to his mother.

Oscar's father was right about the construction. Many of the University's old brick sidewalks were ripped apart. Wider, cement sidewalks were being added.

Great for scooters when they finish, thought Oscar.

At the moment, however, Oscar was dodging construction workers, orange plastic cones, wooden safety barriers, and piles of gravel and paving stones. He imagined himself as one of the finalists for the Gulfstream National Scooter Speed-a-thon.

Riverside Dorm lay another thirty seconds away. Oscar knew the dorm building was full of students celebrating the start of winter break. He also knew that when the neighbors of Room 214 saw him scooter up the hall with bags of Roobick's Cubes, they would realize they needed more blue-tinted ice, too. Oscar's afternoon would fly by with delivery after delivery.

Most customers tipped Oscar for his prompt service. Each tip he earned during winter break placed him another inch closer to his dream: a new scooter. A folding racer with an ultra-light carbon-fiber deck and hypersmooth polyurethane tires. Even ripped-up sidewalks would be no trouble then.

What was that? A flash of neon green caught his eye. A weird bike with red spokeless wheels was speeding toward the Biology Building.

Where had he seen red tires like those before?

Two students on skateboards zoomed in on Oscar's left. One of them veered close. His wheels almost touched the scooter. His arm, tattooed with a red serpent, reached over and grabbed the scooter's handlebars. Oscar could smell garlic pizza on the student's breath.

"Let go!" shouted Oscar.

The student smirked. "Little punks can't steer without help," he said.

Neither Oscar nor the student saw the plastic orange cone until it was too late. *CRASH!* The scooter and the board flew into the air. The next thing Oscar remembered was shakily raising his head from a pile of sand next to the sidewalk. His scooter lay next to him on its side, the back wheel spinning wildly. A thin line of blood gleamed on Oscar's left knee. His hands stung from hitting gravel. *Oh no!* One of the blue Roobick bags had a gash, and a small mound of ice cubes trickled onto the hot cement.

"Look what you did!" yelled Oscar.

The two skateboarders were already gliding away on their boards, laughing and waving at him.

Oscar stood up and straightened his scooter. He scooped most of the melting ice cubes back into the bag and folded the loose plastic over the rip. *What will the guys in Room 214 say when they see the torn bag?* thought Oscar. *They might not pay the full six dollars.* What would his father say?

Oscar wiped the sweat from his eyes. His knee was scraped up. *No big deal.* Ignoring the pain, he kicked off and cruised toward Riverside Dorm.

The hundred-year-old clock tower that stood in the center of the University boomed out the hour. *BONG . . . BONG . . .*

Oscar felt the warm sun on the back of his neck. *Who knows how many seconds I lost because of that stupid skateboarder. Or how much ice I lost!* He needed to make up the lost time.

Wait! That alley behind the Biology Building is a great short-cut.

The banged-up scooter whizzed toward the Bio Building. Two fast turns almost tipped the ice bags off Oscar's deck, but he never lost control. Another burst of speed and Oscar was zooming between the alley's smooth concrete walls.

Another rider on a silver scooter was rocketing toward him.

Is there enough room to pass him? Oscar held his breath and braced both feet on the deck.

He felt the other boy's shirt tail brush against his bare legs. Another second and Oscar had reached the end of the alley. He skidded to a stop and looked behind him. The other kid had done the same. They both couldn't believe their luck. But Oscar knew that avoiding a crash had more to do with skill than luck.

Room 214 sat at the end of a long hall at the top of two flights of carpeted stairs. Oscar's knock was greeted by a tall blond student. He was wearing a red-and-black University of Metroville jersey.

"What took you so long, kid?" he snarled.

Oscar was silent. He hated making excuses.

The blond student picked up the two bags and

threw them to his buddies inside the apartment.

"Hey!" came a yell. "There's ice all over the floor."

Oscar looked down at his sneakers. He hoped the guy would hurry up and give him the money so he could leave.

"That bag's all ripped, kid," said the tall blond.

The door opened wider and the blond student was joined by one of his friends. The friend's arm sported a tattoo. A red serpent. Oscar smelled a whiff of pizza and suddenly his stomach turned into a bag of Roobick's Cubes. It was the student with the skateboard.

The skateboarder looked at Oscar and sneered.

"This kid looks lazy," he said to his friend. "Probably fooled around on his way over here. That's why he's late. And look! He's bleeding all over your floor, man!"

Oscar looked down at his knee. The blood had stopped and was already drying on his leg. There was no blood on the floor.

"Here's five bucks," said the tall blond in the jersey. He shoved a bill in Oscar's face.

"It is six dollars," said Oscar

"Scram!" said the skateboarder. "My friend's not paying full price when you can't even deliver what he ordered."

The door banged shut.

Oscar turned to go. The hall was full of students'

heads curiously poking out their doors, watching him walk by. He was sure he heard some of them laughing.

Outside the dorm, Oscar stared gloomily at the bill in his hand. Only five dollars. And no tip. He was not in a hurry to return to the grocery store and face his parents. His mother would make a fuss over his knee. His father would say something like, "I told you to be careful of the construction." Oscar would not mention the skateboarder. His mother would complain again that it was too dangerous delivering groceries all over campus by scooter. He didn't want her worrying. But he didn't want to stop delivering, either. Besides, making excuses was something a little kid would do.

Oscar fished four quarters out of the pocket where he kept all his tip money. He would add them to the blond kid's five-dollar bill.

As he glided past the Biology Building a second time, Oscar slowed down. He thought he might spy that silver scooter again.

His front tire wobbled slightly as it moved more slowly. *Great! My tire got wrecked in the crash.*

Oscar sighed. How could this day possibly get any worse?

A security guard burst through a doorway in the Bio Building and pointed straight at Oscar. "Stop, thief!" she yelled.

3

CHAMELEON

"C'mon, Speck," said Lily Blue. "Come back down here."

Lily pulled a chair over to a classroom window in the Biology Building. She climbed onto the plastic seat. She reached up with her right hand and gently detached her pet chameleon Speck from the smooth glass. His tiny eyes blinked. His delicate toes flexed, bright apple-green.

"I know, I know," she said, "You want to go outside and ride the scooter some more." Lily petted Speck's tiny head, then stared out the window. *When is Mom going to finish with this building?* she wondered.

Lily's mother worked as a security guard at the University of Metroville. Every day, twice a day, Sharon Blue patrolled the buildings on the east side of the campus. The Bio Building was the last building on her route. Then she would report back to the Security Headquarters, take a ten-minute coffee break, and start all over again, beginning with the

Space Science Center. Right now, Lily's mother was checking out the auditorium on the third floor. She was investigating a suspicious noise.

Classes had ended in the Biology Department. She and Lily were the only people in the building. But when they had reached the second floor, they both had heard a crash upstairs.

"Lily, wait in here," her mother had said.

"I'll be quiet—" Lily began.

"Don't start," said her mother. "You know the rules. You're not even supposed to be in the building with me."

Lily had talked her mother into taking her and Speck on guard duty so they could visit the new exhibit being set up in the Biology building. The exhibit was called THE WORLD'S FIRST DEFENSE TEAM: How Animals Protect Themselves. Lily hoped that she might find exotic chameleons on display. "You might meet some long-lost relatives," she had told Speck. The third floor, where the exhibit was located, was the last floor her mother would patrol. That was also where the noises had come from.

"Sounds like breaking glass," Lily had remarked.

"I have ears," said her mother. "Now shush. Oh, and Speck," she added, petting the tiny green creature that clung to Lily's left ear, "I expect you to guard Lily 'til I get back."

"Careful, Mom," said Lily as her mother shut the door.

Ten minutes had dragged by. Lily heard the hundred-year-old clock tower that stood in the center of the University. *BONG . . . BONG . . .*

Lily knew her mother was smart and could always call for more security guards on her radio if she needed help. That didn't stop Lily from worrying.

As she stood on the plastic chair and stared out the window, Lily said to the squirming Speck now in her fist, "Not much of a view." The window faced the narrow alley that ran between the Bio Building and the building next door. A sudden blink of silver glittered in the alley below. A blond boy was streaking into the alley on a streamlined scooter.

"That's a Hurricane 5000," she whispered to Speck. Lily knew as much about scooters as she did about chameleons. Speck rotated his eye-cones, unimpressed.

A flash of red appeared at the opposite end of the alley.

"That's the kid with the ice," said Lily. Living a few blocks from the University, Lily had often seen the dark-haired boy with the red scooter delivering ice and groceries all over campus. "He's riding a Fireball XL. It has a long footboard, but it's fast."

Lily's grip tightened on Speck. His pink tongue flickered.

"They're going to crash!" she said.

The two scooters rocketed toward each other, neither one of them slowing down.

Lily clamped both hands around the chameleon. *The alley's too narrow,* she thought.

Without thinking, she closed her eyes. Speck's eyes were open. He spied a fly buzzing in circles on the other side of the window. A fat, juicy fly. Like a bolt of green lightning, Speck flashed out of Lily's fist.

"Speck!" Lily opened her eyes. Below, in the alley, the two scooters were now racing away from each other. Both boys had somehow avoided a terrible collision. *Good riders,* thought Lily. *But where's Speck?*

Somewhere, glass was breaking. The auditorium! Lily heard something heavy bumping and twanging down the stairs outside in the hall. Where was her mother! And where was Speck?

The chameleon sat calmly on the windowsill. He had shifted color from green to soft brown, matching the wooden windowsill. The buzzing fly was still tempting Speck from the other side of the glass. A swift dart of his pink tongue, which hadn't changed color, alerted Lily to his new location.

I wish I could do that. Lily scooped up Speck and set him on her left ear. *Changing colors to match my surroundings. It's almost as good as being invisible.*

Speck shot one last hungry glance at the juicy fly as Lily rushed out of the room.

"Lily! I told you to stay inside!" Her mother was running down the steps from the third floor.

"What happened? What was that noise?"

"The exhibit's been broken into," said her mother. Without stopping, she turned and headed down to the first floor. "Follow me." Then she quickly added, "Wait."

The bumping and twanging noise had stopped.

"What was it?" whispered Lily.

"A bike, I think," said her mother. "It rushed past me upstairs. A green-and-red blur. Then I heard it banging down the stairs."

A bicycle in the Bio Building? A bicycle shooting down the stairs would have made those same bumps and twangs that Lily had heard.

"Stay here," said her mother. "I'll go downstairs and have a quick look."

4

THE MISSING
MONKEY-TAIL

"Pat! Pat, are you there?"

Sharon Blue whispered into her two-way radio. She wanted another guard to meet her at the Bio Building.

"Quiet now, Speck," said Lily. As her mother tiptoed down to the first floor, Lily peered up the steps that led to the third-floor auditorium.

What if there's someone else up there? A second thief? Or a whole gang of them? Perhaps someone had hid from her mother in a shadowy corner, waiting for the right moment to escape. Lily patted her left ear, felt Speck still clinging there, then climbed the steps.

A poster at the top of the steps announced:

THE WORLD'S FIRST DEFENSE TEAM

A stone arch next to the poster led into a large airy auditorium. The floor and walls were cool gray marble. A maze of glass display cases were alive with squirming, slithering, swimming, buzzing, and crawling creatures.

Lily saw creatures she recognized and some she had only read about on the Internet. Each case was labeled with the animal's name: Glass Snake . . . Bombardier Beetle . . . Clown Fish . . . Io Moth . . .

Lily's sneakers crunched loudly on broken glass. *Good move, Lily,* she thought. *If there is someone up here, they know I'm up here, too.* The broken glass meant that something else was also wandering around the auditorium. One of the creatures must have escaped. Which one? She stood next to a damaged case that looked like a terrarium. A sunlamp attached to its wire-mesh lid beamed down into a leafy, empty case. Three hard-boiled eggs gleamed in the sunlamp's blaze.

Lily saw a printed card on the floor among the shattered glass. She bent down and read:

SOLOMON ISLAND SKINK
(Also: Monkey-Tailed Skink)
Solomon Islands, Pacific Ocean

"See, Speck?" said Lily, straightening up. "One of your relatives. Just like I said. But those eggs look weird." She peered closer at the hard-boiled eggs. "Is that sugar?" she said. All three eggs were sprinkled with bits of shiny glass.

"If there's glass on the inside of the case, then someone smashed into it from the outside," said Lily to Speck. "This is what Mom meant when she said the exhibit was broken into. But why would someone steal a skink?"

"Lily!" Her mother's voice bounced up the stairwell.

Speck scampered to the safety of Lily's ear. Lily snatched up the typewritten card and retreated down the steps. Before she reached the bottom, however, she heard a heavy bang. Then another. *The front doors*, she thought.

She found her mother outside, flying down the stone steps that led from the doors to the sidewalk below. "Stop, thief!" her mother yelled.

Lily saw her mother point at a familiar dark-haired boy. The Ice Boy on the ruby-red scooter. He wore a bright green T-shirt. The two colors must have reminded her mother of the blur she had seen inside the Bio Building.

"Come over here," commanded her mother. The dark-haired boy stood still. A fierce, scared expression clouded his face. It looked to Lily as if the boy was trying to decide whether to run or stay. He had one foot on the deck of his scooter, and the other foot poised to kick off.

"What were you doing in the building?" demanded Sharon Blue.

The boy was silent.

"But, Mom!" said Lily.

Her mother silenced her with a wave of a hand. "Not now, Lily."

"But it couldn't have been him," said Lily. "I saw him outside."

Sharon Blue turned to face her daughter. "What are you talking about?"

"When I was waiting for you," explained Lily. "I saw him"—she pointed at the boy. "He was in the alley behind the building. He and another boy were riding scooters."

"What's your name?" asked Sharon Blue.

"Oscar," said the boy. "Oscar Santiago."

"From Santiago Market?" asked Sharon.

Oscar nodded.

"What were you doing in the alley?"

"Taking a shortcut," said Oscar. "I was delivering ice to Riverside Dorm."

"I saw him, Mom," said Lily. "He was outside when I heard the glass breaking upstairs."

Sharon's voice softened as she said to Oscar, "Good thing you have a witness, young man. I apologize."

"Two witnesses," grinned Lily. She patted her left ear.

Oscar caught a glimpse of something small and green moving in the girl's hair.

Sharon Blue's radio suddenly squawked. Sharon listened carefully to the report from one of her fellow security guards. "It's over by the bridge," she said to Lily.

Lily and Oscar, out of curiosity, both followed Sharon toward the River Bridge. Halfway to the bridge, a blond boy on a gleaming silver Hurricane scooter shimmered past them on the sidewalk. Oscar saw the boy wink.

"That was the other scooter," said Lily.

"I've seen that boy before," said her mother. "I think his father is a professor."

Lily turned to Oscar, as he slowly propelled his scooter alongside her. "That reminds me," she said. "How did you—?"

"Not crash?" asked Oscar. "Well, you have to know what you're doing."

"I have a Double-Z Stingray," said Lily. "I know how to ride. And I was sure you were going to crash into that other kid."

"Luck," said Oscar.

"Skill," said Lily, smiling. Then she added, "Actually, I closed my eyes."

Oscar chuckled. "I did, too."

Speck, still clinging to Lily's ear, pointed his eye-cones at Oscar's scooter. The chameleon stared at the scuff marks, the wobbly front wheel, and the cut on Oscar's knee.

They also passed one of the teachers from the Biology Building. Lily recognized her as Miss Cruz.

"I already talked with your partner back there,"

said Miss Cruz wearily to Lily's mother. She pointed toward the Mixaloopi River Bridge.

"You saw the thief?" said Sharon Blue.

"Just a glimpse," Miss Cruz said.

"When were you in the building?" asked Sharon.

Miss Cruz was sweating and breathing hard. "I'm tired, I think I need to sit down. Could you ask me these questions later?"

They watched the teacher walk off toward the Bio Building.

At the River Bridge, Lily, her mother, and Oscar met the skinny security guard that had talked with Max Martin. *He's as skinny as a skink,* thought Lily. The guard was the Pat that Sharon Blue had called on her radio from the Biology Building. He filled her in on the details of the vanishing bicycle. He read her the statements made by Max, the two students on the bridge, and the girl who had been sitting and reading on the bench. He also told her what the guards on the other end of the bridge had *not* seen.

Lily spied the two students, the pink-haired boy and the black-haired girl, exiting the walkway. They were walking toward the bus stop below the bridge.

"Where's that other girl you interviewed?" asked Sharon Blue.

The skinny, pale guard blinked at the empty bench. "She's gone," he said.

"And you didn't get her name?" asked Sharon.

Pat flipped nervously through the pages of his notebook.

"She's vanished like the missing bike," said Oscar to Lily.

"Or she blended in with the background," Lily said. "Like a chameleon."

5

THE THREE CLUES

"Sorry I'm late, Dad," said Max, skidding to a stop alongside his father's parked car.

"What's that?" His father was sitting in the car, windows rolled down, reading a thick hardcover book. Max saw a picture of a swirling galaxy on the front cover. "You're late?" His father glanced at his wristwatch. "Oh yeah, I guess you are. Sorry, Maxwell, I got caught up in this book. It's all about giant solar systems grinding through space and—"

"Dad, can a bike turn invisible?"

"What?"

"Turn invisible. Disappear. Vanish."

"Are you asking me if it's scientifically possible?"

"No, not scientific," said Max. "I mean in real life. Because I saw it happen. What I mean is, I *didn't* see it happen."

"Didn't see what, Max?"

"The bike vanish before my eyes."

Mr. Martin closed his book and set it on his lap.

"Okay, Max, give me the story. Twenty-five words or less."

Max took a deep breath and told his father all about the mysterious vanishing bike. He described the bike's weird tires, the skinny security guard, and the students walking on the River Bridge. He told how the bike disappeared between the eastern end of the bridge's walkway and the western end.

"That was thirty-one words, Max."

"And I almost collided with another kid on a scooter," added Max.

"Almost?"

"Dad, if I'm traveling fast enough on my scooter," said Max, "is it possible, I mean, *scientifically possible*, for me to slide through a wall? Without crashing?"

His father pinched his nose and looked thoughtful. "Well . . . maybe you could, if you were traveling at the speed of light."

"Could I slide through another scooter?"

"Max, do you know how fast you'd have to be moving? One hundred eighty-six thousand miles per second!"

"So the answer is no, huh?" asked Max.

"You never told me what the thief on the so-called vanishing bike stole," said Mr. Martin.

"Um, that lady's purse, I guess," said Max. "She never did say." Max realized that the skinny guard hadn't mentioned what the thief had stolen, either.

The guard had asked questions only about the disappearing bike.

Mr. Martin started his car's engine. "Maybe we'll hear about it on the evening news," he said. "Ready to race?"

"Yup," said Max. He tightened his grip on the Hurricane's handlebars.

Each day that his father taught at the Space Science Center, Max would meet him after class in the Center's parking lot. Then they would race to see which vehicle would reach home first, the car or the scooter. Mr. Martin could obviously travel faster than Max, but only as fast as the speed limit allowed. He was also limited to streets. Max's scooter could speed over sidewalks, alleys, and walkways. Since their house lay only five blocks away, Max felt it was a fair race. Especially since he and his scooter had already won twice that week.

Max's favorite part of his route lay back on the River Bridge. Zooming along the wide sidewalk on the lower level, Max could watch the sunlight reflecting off the Mixaloopi, far below to his right. On his left side, trucks, SUVs, and motorcycles made a cool breeze that rippled against his arms and legs. The traffic thrummed like waves of water pounding on the Gulf's beach.

As Max neared the entrance to the bridge, he glided by a bus stop full of students. He saw the teenage boy that the skinny guard had interviewed. It was easy to pick out the pink hair in a crowd. The boy was talking to his girl friend in the army pants. A second girl, struggling with a heavy backpack, stood next to them. *That's the girl from the bench*, thought Max. *They must be talking about the vanishing bike.* All three of them were laughing, but as Max's scooter rolled by, the pink-haired boy scowled at him.

What's his problem? wondered Max. *Maybe his nose stud is screwed too tight.*

* * *

"It's getting late," said Miss Cruz. She balanced a towering stack of final-exam papers in her arms.

Lily and her mother had returned to the Bio Building. They met Miss Cruz on her way down the front steps.

"Sorry to trouble you, Miss Cruz," said Sharon Blue.

"Then don't," said Miss Cruz. "I have a lot of work to do. Excuse me."

Lily pulled out the typewritten card from her pocket. "Why would someone steal a skink, Miss Cruz?"

Miss Cruz stared suspiciously at Lily.

"Why do you say that?" she asked.

"Because that's what was stolen, right?" said

Lily. "It's missing from its case upstairs in the auditorium."

Miss Cruz dropped her exams like a load of old laundry. Sheets of paper spilled over the steps. The teacher spun on her heels and bolted inside the building. Lily and her mother exchanged a quick glance and then also ran inside. Miss Cruz was sprinting up the stairs toward the auditorium. By the time Lily and her mother reached the top step, they heard Miss Cruz's cries echoing under the huge dome.

"This is terrible! Terrible!"

Sharon Blue was confused. "I thought you knew this happened. I saw the broken glass up here earlier and figured that's why you were upset. Didn't you tell the other guard about the theft?"

"My gradebook was stolen," said Miss Cruz. "I didn't know about this!" Her shoes crunched on the broken glass as she paced back and forth. "This is absolutely terrible. Now I have to call the dean." She grabbed her ponytail in frustration, and Lily feared she was going to pull it out by its roots.

"When did the thief steal your gradebook?" asked Sharon Blue.

"When I yelled for help," Miss Cruz said frantically. "It's the guide for all my exams. Now I'll have to spend hours figuring out students' grades all over again."

She explained to Lily and her mother that she

had entered the Bio Building around two o'clock, her normal office hour. At the same time, Lily and her mother were on the upper floors, Lily remembered hearing the clock tower bong twice. Miss Cruz said she had come to pick up some exams that needed grading during the winter break. The students always dropped off their work using her office door's mail slot. And while she was in her office gathering papers, Miss Cruz heard several strange bumps in the hall. She stepped out of her office and was almost run down by a strange bike.

"Whoever rode that bike stole the gradebook I was still carrying in my hand," said Miss Cruz. "It happened so quickly, I didn't get a look at the rider's face."

That's when Miss Cruz ran outside, chasing the strange bike, and instead met Max Martin riding his silver Hurricane, and the other guard Lily's mother had called on her radio.

"That's when we left the building, too," said Sharon.

"And saw Ice Boy," said Lily.

"Ice Boy?" asked her mother.

"You know . . . Oscar," said Lily. "That's what the students call him."

Miss Cruz examined the broken display cases. "Only the Monkey-Tail was taken. Strange. It's not a very valuable creature. The Blue-Tongued Skink and the Soa-Soa are worth more."

"Soa-Soa?" asked Lily.

"It's a lizard about three feet long. We're borrowing it from a zoo in Indonesia," explained Miss Cruz. "They're a threatened species."

Lily noticed a black-and-yellow flutter from inside a nearby cage. "What's a monarch butterfly doing in the exhibit?" asked Lily. "I didn't think they protected themselves in any special way."

Miss Cruz grinned. "It tricked you," she said. "It's not a monarch, it's a viceroy butterfly. Monarch butterflies taste bitter to birds, but viceroys taste sweet. Over the years, the viceroys that looked more like monarchs were able to survive."

"A clever disguise," said Sharon Blue.

"A life-saving disguise," added Miss Cruz.

Lily realized that chameleons were not the only experts in camouflage. Blending in with your surroundings, like Speck, was one way to hide. But looking like something else, like the viceroy, was an even smarter trick.

* * *

"Why so late?" asked Oscar's father as the boy parked his damaged scooter inside the store's back door. Then Mr. Santiago noticed his son's knee. "Are you all right?"

"Fine, Papi." Oscar plopped down on a plastic

carton. His father and two brothers, Ernesto and Carlos, stood glaring at him. They stood in front of a huge ROOBICK'S CUBES' cooler. From where Oscar sat, all he could read between their angry faces and folded arms was ROB CUBS.

"There was a robbery," said Oscar.

"Robbery!" His father's jaw dropped. "You were robbed? Ernesto, Carlos! Run and get the police."

"No, no, not me," said Oscar. "Some teacher at the University. Here." He handed his father the five-dollar bill and four quarters for the Riverside Dorm ice bags.

"But so late," his father repeated.

"I . . . I was a witness," said Oscar. He was afraid of saying too much. If he told his father that he had been mistaken for the thief himself, his father would grow angrier.

"Hey, *muchacho*, what happened to your wheels?" said Ernesto. Oscar's older brother was examining the red scooter's front tire.

"Uh, the construction," said Oscar. "There's dirt and sand and barriers all over the place."

"See?" said his father. "Construction! What did I tell you?"

Ernesto knelt down by the Fireball, sitting back on his workboots. "Carlos," he said. "Get my tools out of the back of the truck."

Mr. Santiago took a step closer. "You think you can fix it?" he asked.

"*Sí*, Papi. Looks like a pin was knocked loose."

"Thanks, Ernesto," said Oscar.

"Don't take all day," ordered their father. "This is a grocery store, not a repair shop. We have work to do, customers to keep happy. Oscar, you have more deliveries. And I need you to be more careful. It's eggs this time."

"*Huevos?*" asked Oscar.

His father nodded. "Students asking for dozens and dozens of eggs. Not frozen pizzas, not frozen burritos. Eggs! I hope no one is getting their windows splattered by some wise guys tonight. Boys, let me know as soon as that bike is fixed."

"Scooter," corrected Oscar.

"Whatever," said his father, throwing up his hands.

Ernesto tapped his finger against his new mustache. "It's a good thing this is not a bike," he said. "A bike's wheels would have been more damaged. These little tires are metal."

Carlos set down a toolbox next to the scooter.

"*Sí*," Carlos agreed. "Your tire would be flat."

Flat? Oscar saw the strange bike in his mind again. Those peculiar reddish wheels. Now he knew what they had reminded him of.

Balloons.

6

SPIES AND SHADOWS

"Looks like a balloon, doesn't it, Speck?"

Lily and Speck stared up at the full yellow moon hanging over the Gulf. They were both sitting on their front porch. Sharon Blue was busy in the kitchen, making fudge and baking cookies for the upcoming holidays. Lily stared down at a blank pad of paper. She was trying to make sense of the mysterious vanishing bicycle. Speck squatted on the pad, blinking importantly. Lily chewed the cap of her pen. The smell of the fudge made her hungry.

Earlier that night she had spent an hour searching the Internet for information on Solomon Island skinks. She discovered the skinks were extremely picky eaters. They prefered hibiscus blossoms, pothos plants, and hard-boiled eggs. But they wouldn't eat a hibiscus two days in a row. Solomon Islanders liked variety in their meals.

Maybe a giant chameleon ate the thief and the bike and is living on the roof of the River Bridge walkway. Lily shook her head. *That's just the fudge getting to me.*

Lily thought back to everything she had heard and seen after the mysterious bike zoomed down the stairs inside the Biology Building. She also remembered what the guard Pat had told her mother while they stood on the River Bridge. Lily wrote a list of names.

Who They Were	What They Saw
Lily (me)	Nothing
Mom	A green-and-red blur
Miss Cruz	Thinks it was a bike
Oscar, the Ice Boy	A flash of green and red by the Bio Bldg
The blond kid with the silver scooter	Saw the bike go into the east end of the River Bridge walkway, then turned around
Other security guard (Mom says his name is Pat)	Nothing, got there too late

Girl on bench	Saw bike rush past her
Pink-haired boy	Saw bike enter walkway from the east and then rush past him (going west) Says he heard squealing down on street below
Dark-haired girl	Saw same thing as her boyfriend Didn't hear anything unusual
Guards on west bank	Nothing

"Sorry, Speck," said Lily. "I guess I should put your name down, too." She added:

Speck (alias Spectrum)	Nothing, or else he's not talking

The chameleon had turned a shade of canary green, trying hard to match the yellow of Lily's notepad. He goggled his eyes at the strange marks on the paper, rotated them twice, then blinked his approval.

"That's at least ten or eleven humans who were witnesses," said Lily. "And one reptile. Only four people really saw the bike—the students on the bridge and that kid on the Hurricane. But no one got a description of the thief. I suppose it doesn't matter if the rider of the bike was a girl or a guy. The most important thing is *how* the bike disappeared."

Earlier in the evening, Lily and her mother had watched the news on TV. News of the theft and the strange bicycle was the top story on all the channels. *But they didn't mention that the bike vanished,* Lily thought. *Why not? Didn't want to scare people from using the bridge?* The University was offering a reward of five hundred dollars for information about the missing skink and gradebook. "That could buy a new scooter," Lily had said to Speck. "Two scooters."

To Lily, the money was not as important as her mother's job. If she could solve the mystery and give her mom the credit, Sharon Blue would become a hero. Lily's mother could get promoted to supervisor. Her mother had been talking about the new job opening for weeks. *She'd be good as a supervisor. She likes giving orders.*

Lily gazed down at the tiny reptile that slowly crawled across her notepad. Then she looked up at the yellow moon.

Paper, moon, and Speck (partly) were all the same color. Yellow.

Maybe the weird bike did some sort of chameleon trick after all, thought Lily.

She sniffed the air. Her mother was still making fudge. Lily deposited Speck in the pocket of her sweatshirt, then she quietly tiptoed down the porch's sidesteps and retrieved her scooter from the side of the house. *I'll only be gone a few minutes. Mom won't even notice.*

The River Bridge gleamed white as a bone in the moonlight. Lily raced her gold-and-black Stingray in the cool, open air on the bridge's upper level, between the covered walkway and the railing. Far below glistened the surface of the wide Mixaloopi. A second moon hung reflected in the water. She braked the Stingray in the middle of the bridge. Only the hum of traffic on the lower level broke the silence. The campus was deserted.

"Keep your eyes open, Speck," she said. "Look for a good hiding place."

The breeze blew her hair in front of her eyes as she slowly strolled along the bridge. Nothing looked like a hiding place large enough for a bike. Inside the covered walkway low concrete benches lay every twenty feet. Outside, on the open bridge, old-fashioned lampposts lit Lily's path.

Lily walked eastward, in the direction of the Bio Building.

Something light touched her shoulder. "Get back up on my ear, Speck," she said. "Why can't you stay put—"

Another tap on her shoulder. A person's hand.

"Gosh, you scared me!" said Lily.

The kid on the Hurricane 5000 stood right behind her. His blond hair was hidden under a black baseball cap turned backward on his head. "What are you doing out here?" he asked.

Lily gazed at him and folded her arms. "Same thing you are, I'll bet," she said. "Looking for clues."

"Clues?"

"Yeah, for the bike that disappeared."

"Maybe I am," admitted Max.

"You saw it, didn't you?" said Lily. "You saw the whole thing."

Max nodded. "But I didn't see how it disappeared."

"Think it was a trapdoor?" asked Lily.

"Why? Because that pink-haired guy heard squealing tires down on the street? Nah, I haven't found anything that looks like an escape hatch."

Lily agreed. The steel and concrete bridge was rock-solid.

"Think the bike bungee-jumped over the side of the bridge?" said Max.

"The guards would have seen it," said Lily. *Unless it pulled a viceroy trick, and looked like something else,* she thought.

Lily stared at the walkway's roof. "Think it could be up there" she asked.

"I haven't checked that out yet," said Max. "Hey, what's that?" He pointed to Lily's handlebars.

Lily laughed. "That's just Speck," she said. "Short for Spectrum. He changes colors."

"Cool name." Max gently stroked the apple-green reptile's tail, as it clung to the Stingray's handlebars. "I've never seen a chameleon up close before," he said.

"I like the clock on your handlebars," said Lily. "That's a Hurricane 5000, right?"

"Yup. Hey, that gives me an idea. Let's time how long it takes to cross the bridge."

"Good idea. Let's time it for riding *and* for walking."

A few minutes later, Lily and Max caught their breaths at the eastern edge of the River Bridge. They sat on the same cement bench where the young woman reading the paperback had sat earlier in the day. It had taken them two and one-half minutes to cross the bridge by walking. Kicking their scooters as fast as they could, they covered the same distance in forty seconds.

"Your Stingray's pretty fast," said Max, admiringly.

"It's the driver that makes it fast," said Lily. "Real athletes ride scooters."

Max couldn't wait to tell Dylan the newest item he added to his list:

4. Scooter riders are better athletes—male *and* female.

"The thief was probably racing as fast as we were," said Lily. "He must have been on the bridge for about thirty seconds before he—or she—turned invisible."

"My dad says it's scientifically impossible for a bike to disappear," he said.

"Speck can disappear," said Lily. She felt the chameleon crawling around in her sweatshirt pocket. He had scurried inside during the speed timings.

"That's different," said Max. "Speck's not invisible. He blends in."

"Maybe that's what the bike did," suggested Lily. "Blended in with the surroundings."

"Yeah, but how?" asked Max. "There's nothing on the bridge but steel and cement and some glass windows and a few benches."

"It could disguise itself as one part of the bridge," said Lily.

"Or could a bike go so fast that no one would see it?" wondered Max.

"Could it fly?" Lily looked up at the moon. It was whiter than before and hung in the western half of the sky. "There must be something we're forgetting."

Voices.

"Who's that?" whispered Max.

Lily tilted her head. "Students? No, wait! That one voice, the guy's voice, it sounds familiar."

Max nodded. "I recognize it, too."

Two shadows were walking hand in hand inside the walkway. Their voices echoed hollowly on the lonely bridge. "They're coming this way," squeaked Lily.

She and Max pushed their scooters down the ramp that led from the walkway to the sidewalk below. A row of azalea bushes bordered the sidewalk. The two riders pushed their scooters past the thick clumps and crouched down to spy.

"Now *we're* the chameleons," said Max.

Two pairs of shoes scraped on the cement as the shadows descended the ramp. Max could smell sweet perfume.

"Your scooter is on my foot!" said Lily.

"No, it's not," said Max. "It's sitting over here, on my other side."

"Then how . . . ?" Lily turned and saw a third scooter hidden among the azaleas. A ruby red scooter.

Oscar put his finger to his lips. "Shhh! They're right out there," he whispered.

The shadows had stopped in front of the bushes and the three spies.

I knew it! thought Max. *That's the skinny guard from this afternoon.*

Lily squinted through the branches. *That's Pat! But who's the girl?*

"That's the girl from the bridge," Max whispered to the others. "She was reading a book on the bench up there when the bike rushed into the walkway."

"Well, she's not reading now," said Lily, squirming.

"I hope they're not going to kiss," said Oscar. The three spies turned to look at each other and silently mouthed: "Eewwww!"

7

THE YO-YO GUY

"Do you hear something?" said Pat.

The girl moved away from him and stood still, listening. "Only your keys," she said.

Lily was crouching low in the bushes, trying hard to keep from laughing. Oscar held his hands tightly over his mouth. Max chewed on his black baseball cap.

The girl gulped nervously and said, "I thought I heard something . . . *slither.*"

"Oh, Brenda, you're thinking about that missing skink," said Pat.

"You bet I am," said Brenda. "What did you call it again? A monkey something-or-other?"

"A Monkey-Tailed Skink," said Pat. "It has a long, thick tail like a monkey and can pull itself up into tree branches when it's attacked."

Pat still wore his uniform and, whenever he moved, his keys jangled at his belt. Keys, thought Lily. He has keys to the locked Bio Building. That's how the thief got inside the auditorium.

The girl shuddered. "I hate lizards." She looked up into the dark, inky branches of a nearby tree. "Think it could be around here?" she asked.

Pat chuckled. "I wouldn't worry about that little skink."

"Little? You said it was over three feet long!"

"That skink is nowhere near us," said Pat. "I can tell you—"

Behind the azalea bushes, a green reptilian head poked out from Lily's sweatshirt. Oscar shouted, "What's that?" and tumbled backward onto the grass.

Brenda screamed, startled by Oscar's shout. Speck, frightened by Oscar's sudden movement and cry, leaped to safety. Speck's idea of safety at that moment was something larger than Oscar— solid, and unmoving. Like a security guard.

Speck made a four-point landing on Pat's chin. The guard screamed at the top of his lungs, startling his girlfriend a second time, and he started smacking at his chin. Speck jumped again, unhurt, while Pat slapped himself in the face. Looking for a quieter and lower spot, Speck next landed on Brenda's sandaled foot. This new haven was no better than the last. The girl frantically tried to kick Speck off her foot without having to touch him. Speck flew off, but Brenda managed to strike Pat at least twice in his shins.

Lily breathlessly watched Speck's travels like a

spectator watching a tennis match. She gripped her Stingray's handlebars with both hands and kicked with all her strength. She shot across the sidewalk and dodged the skinny guard as he bounced along the sidewalk in pain, clutching his chin with one hand and a shin with the other. Brenda had fallen onto the grass and was looking for her missing sandal that had flown into the air and landed on the other side of the azalea bushes. Lily scooped up Speck from the ground and zoomed toward the bridge.

"Stop, thief!" yelled Brenda. "Bring back my shoe!"

Oscar and Max appeared magically at Lily's side. All three spies raced toward the lower level of the River Bridge.

Cold air washed against their faces, knees, and knuckles.

"Good work, Agent Stingray," joked Max.

"Ice Boy was the one who shouted," said Lily, defensively.

"You had a snake on you," said Oscar.

"He's not a snake, he's a chameleon," said Lily.

"Whatever," said Oscar.

"We sure blended in with our surroundings, huh?" said Max. "I bet they never knew we were there."

Lily had to grin at that.

"I don't like being called a thief," said Oscar. "Twice in one day!"

"We can tell my mom," Lily called over her shoulder. "She'll straighten it out with Pat."

In fact, thought Lily, as the three of them neared the west bank of the Mixaloopi River, *that looks like Mom now.*

Sharon Blue had pulled her car up onto the curb at the end of the bridge. She stood, hands on hips, staring at the approaching trio.

"Lily! What on earth . . . "

Lily skidded the Stingray to a stop. "Mom! We were only looking for clues!"

"And scaring poor Pat's girlfriend to death," said her mother.

Lily felt sick. "How do you know—?"

"Pat called me on his cell phone," said Sharon. "Luckily, I was on my way over here. When I noticed you missing from the house, young lady, I knew you'd be snooping around the campus. Looking for clues, as you call it."

"It's not her fault," said Max.

"It was that snake," said Oscar.

"Chameleon," said Lily.

Sharon shook her head. "Speck is out here, too? Lily! How could you do this?"

Lily stared down at her scooter's wheels. "We were trying to help. I thought if you discovered the crook, you might get a promotion."

"That girl was the one who saw the bike," added Max. "Why would she be so friendly all of a sudden with that guard? I'll bet they planned the robbery together."

"They're on a date," said Sharon Blue.

"But this afternoon they acted like they never met before," said Max.

"They hadn't," said Sharon. "That's what a date is for, young man. Getting to know someone. During his investigation this afternoon, Pat found out who the girl was, and I guess he asked her out. I don't know why I'm standing here with you kids. Into the car."

"We can scooter home," Oscar said, weakly.

"Forget it. I will drive you boys home." Lily's mother opened the trunk of her car. Each of the spies pressed the catches on their scooters that allowed the handlebar-stands to fold down. Like most scooters, these were collapsible and fit easily into the trunk.

"Number Five," said Max. "Motorcycles cannot be folded."

"What did you say?" asked Lily.

Max's face burned bright red. "Uh, just making a list," he said.

Once the boys gave Lily's mother their addresses, the three children sat silently in the backseat. Even Speck lay quietly in Lily's palm, afraid to move.

Sharon Blue finally spoke up.

"I'll talk to Pat in the morning. And you kids should apologize to him in person."

"Apologize?" groaned Lily. "But it was a mistake."

"Which is exactly why you should apologize," said her mother. "You must have scared that poor girl out of her mind. And he said you took her shoe."

"We did not take her shoe," said Lily, angrily. Now she knew how Oscar felt, being accused of something she didn't do. "It flew off her foot."

"Her shoe just flew off by itself?" demanded her mother.

"She was trying to get . . . uh, something off her foot," said Oscar.

"It did look pretty funny," said Max eagerly. Then he added, "Sorry."

"We thought they were guilty," explained Lily. "That's the only reason we were watching them. I mean, Pat has keys to all the buildings. And besides those two students walking to the bus stop, she was the only other person on the bridge."

Sharon Blue coughed. "Since Pat has keys—as you point out—why would he steal something from Miss Cruz's office at the same time he knew she'd be there? And Pat's friend was *not* the only other person on the bridge. I spoke with some of the other guards tonight." Lily knew it. Her mother was as interested in solving this mystery as she was. And she knew her mom wanted that promotion.

"Who else was up there?" asked Lily.

"A male student was waiting for his friends on the west bank side. The guards saw him yo-yoing over there."

"People still yo-yo?" asked Lily.

"The young man didn't see anything. He said he'd been waiting there for about fifteen minutes, practicing his yo-yo. Until the guards showed up, he said he was alone the whole time."

"The whole time?" asked Max. "Are you sure?"

Sharon Blue nodded. "That's what he told the guards."

Max's eyes grew wide with excitement. He sat back and said, in a low voice only Lily and Oscar could hear, "I think I know who did it."

"Aliens?" asked Lily.

Oscar, who had been silently brooding about the three scooters in the trunk, nodded to himself. Then he whispered to Lily and Max, "And I think I know how it was done!"

8

THE DRAGON'S DEN

The hundred-year-old clock tower stood in the center of the University campus.

BONG . . . BONG . . . BONG . . .

In front of the tall brick structure lay a large circular plot of green lawn. In the middle of the grassy plot, listening to the clock tower bonging out nine o'clock in the morning, the three spies had gathered with their scooters.

Earlier that morning, Lily's mother had made her phone the two boys to meet her at the University. "You can all apologize to Pat," said Sharon Blue. "He starts work at eight."

But Lily had other plans. She told Oscar and Max to meet her instead in front of the clock tower on their scooters. "We can apologize to Pat later," Max suggested.

Sitting on the grassy plot in front of the clock tower, Lily pointed at Max and said, "Okay, what was that crack you made last night about knowing who the thief was?"

She was surprised when both boys began spilling out ideas.

"Slow down!" she cried.

"The weird bike was collapsible," said Oscar. "Like our scooters fitting in the back of your mom's car. The wheels on that weird bike looked like balloons, so I'll bet even those collapse."

"Deflate," said Max.

"Whatever," said Oscar.

"So the bike could be pulled apart and fit into a much smaller space," said Lily. "But which space?"

"The bike pulled a chameleon trick. Like you said last night on the bridge," Max told Lily. "It blended in with the surroundings."

"Which surroundings?" Lily said. "You said there was only steel and windows and benches and—"

It hit her! The other thing she always saw on the bridge. Students. And what were students always carrying?

"Backpacks," said Max. "The bike could be pulled apart and collapsed—"

"Or deflated," said Oscar.

"Yeah, um, deflate. And it could fit into a backpack. Or two."

The pink-haired boy and the girl in the army pants.

"But what makes you sure it's them?" asked Lily.

"Remember what your Mom said last night in the car?" said Max. "About that kid with the yo-yo?"

"He was all alone," said Oscar.

"Right!" said Max. "The yo-yo guy said he'd been waiting for his friends for fifteen minutes. And all he saw were the guards."

"So?" said Lily.

"So . . . if the pink-haired guy and his girlfriend were walking from that direction, then the yo-yo guy should have seen them walk into the walkway. But he didn't."

"They said they were in a hurry to get to the bus stop on the other side," added Lily.

Max nodded. "If they were in a hurry, they should have entered the walkway from the west side, the yo-yo guy's side, and kept walking. It only takes about two or three minutes, right? But the yo-yo guy never saw them."

"They came from the *east* side," said Lily.

"One of them did," said Oscar. "Only one of them rode the bike."

"The other one was waiting for the bike inside the walkway," said Max. "Who knows how long that person had been in there! Then along comes the thief—chased by me—who zips into the walkway and meets his partner. The two of them pull the bike apart, stuff it into their backpacks, and then turn around, pretending to walk back in the direction of the Bio Building."

"Didn't that security guard check their back-packs?" asked Oscar.

"I don't think the skinny guy did," said Max.

"Even if he had, all he'd see were pieces," said Lily. "He might not recognize it all pulled apart." Lily remembered waiting in the empty Biology classroom yesterday with Speck. The little reptile had hidden in plain sight, inches from her nose. She hadn't recognized him because she was looking for a green Speck instead of a brown one.

"The students would probably lie and say the parts were something else," suggested Oscar. "Like the wheels were balloons for a dorm party."

"Or the handlebars were part of a table," said Max.

"Or part of a class project," said Lily.

Before she left the house that morning, Lily had glanced at her mother's notepad from work. Sharon Blue had jotted down the students' names when Pat gave her his report on the bridge yesterday. Lily copied down their names and the subjects they were majoring in. The pink-haired boy and his girlfriend were both Art majors.

During their huddle on the grassy plot, each of them had supplied a valuable piece of the puzzle. Who, how, and where. The pieces fit like a newly assembled bike. Now it was time for action.

"And if we don't hurry, that skink could get sick and die," said Lily. "I was reading about it on the

Internet, and those lizards are really finicky when it comes to eating. The thief might not know what to feed it."

"What does it eat?" asked Max.

"Plants mostly," said Lily. "And eggs and—"

"Eggs?" said Oscar.

"Yeah, hardboiled," added Lily.

Now Oscar knew more than ever that they were on the right trail.

"Of course, some eat pinkies—" said Lily.

"They eat your little finger?" asked Max.

Lily shook her head. "Pinkies are hairless, baby mice. You know, pink. And a really good source of protein, too."

"I think I'm gonna be sick," said Oscar.

"Let's go, the Art Center is over there," Max pointed.

Max, Lily, and Oscar mounted their scooters and steered toward a gleaming pile of steel, glass, and aluminum.

"My dad hates it," said Max. "He says it looks like a pregnant disco ball."

A long, curving ramp that sloped deep into the ground circled the disco ball like a moat. At the lower end of the ramp lay a shiny brass door.

"I think this leads to the workshops," said Max.

"I hope you're right," said Oscar. He was thinking about the new scooter he could buy with the five hundred dollar reward money.

Lily stared at their reflections in the polished brass. Max wore a red U. of M. baseball cap. Oscar wore a bright blue T-shirt with ice cubes printed on the front. She was wearing black-and-gold sunglasses that matched her scooter.

"I hope you're both right," said Lily. She opened the door and led the way inside.

"Yow!" exclaimed Max.

The inside walls were polished aluminum. The red cap, the blue tee shirt, and the sunglasses were reflected back at them from dozens of curious angles.

"It *is* like a disco ball," said Lily. The three spies wandered the mirrored, mazelike hallways for what seemed like an hour. Curving halls led to straight halls. Straight halls led to zig-zag halls. The floor sometimes ramped up, sometimes sloped down. Every door they found was locked. Finally, Oscar said, "*¡Mire!* There!" A gold sign with the word WORKSHOPS and an arrow pointed to the right.

Quietly they glided down the hall.

BANG! BANG!

"Gunshots?" asked Oscar.

Max shook his head. The bangs grew louder as they approached a set of steel double doors.

"It's coming from inside," said Oscar.

The metallic banging was joined by the banter of boys' voices.

"The pink-haired guy?" asked Lily.

The cut on Oscar's knee started to sting. *I know that voice,* he thought.

"Follow me when I count three," said Max.

"You mean, like in the movies?" said Lily.

He silenced her with a wave of his hand. "One," he said, carefully gripping the iron handle.

"Two . . ." The door swung open silently.

"Three!" Max, with the grace of a chameleon, swiftly slipped inside. Lily and Oscar were right on his heels.

The workshop was a long rectangular room with a low ceiling. Machinery and worktables filled up half the space. The banging sounds came from the center of the room. Two male students were building what Max guessed was a bizarre modern sculpture. The pink-haired student hammered while the other student, a stranger to Max, wore safety goggles and operated a welding torch. The torch sizzled and sputtered, flashing like miniature fireworks. The students, concentrating on their work, had not noticed the three spies enter the room behind them.

Lily and Max ducked under a heavy metal table. Oscar darted behind a giant drill press.

"What's that supposed to be?" Lily asked. "Modern art?"

"Modern art with handlebars," said Max.

Lily noticed the strange metal shapes of the sculpture. Handlebars, pedals, gears. *Clever,* she thought. *They're turning the evidence into a piece of art. No one will recognize it. But where's the Solomon Island skink?*

The pink-haired student dropped his hammer with a sudden clang. It bounced and skittered across the floor, landing inches from Oscar's hiding place.

The other student turned down the torch flame. "What's your problem?" he snarled.

"Sorry. It's hot in here," said the pink-haired student. He flapped the sides of his bowling shirt to fan his chest. "I need a soda."

"Then shut up and sit down. I'm almost finished."

The pink-haired student sat heavily onto a nearby stool. "Maybe I should call Ellen and see how she's doing."

"Will you shut up and quit worrying. You sound like an old woman!"

"Listen, Rake—" started the other.

The welder, Rake, threw off his goggles. "Do you want to get caught or not? I told you to steal just the gradebook from Cruz. That was all! If I don't pass her dumb class, my dad's not paying for school anymore. But you had to go and take that flying monkey lizard for your stupid girlfriend!"

"Monkey-Tailed skink," said the other. "And maybe if you paid attention more to what people said, you'd be able to pass your precious class."

The door opened. The inky-haired girl from the

bridge strolled in. She jerked a thumb over her shoulder. "Whose scooters in the hall? They're cool."

Rake hadn't heard her. As soon as he saw her walk in, he turned away and started welding a another bicycle piece to the sculpture.

"Hey, Ellen," said the pink-haired boy.

"Hey, Pinky," said the girl.

Pinky? thought Oscar. He noticed the girl was carrying an old canvas bag. She plopped it on the pink-haired student's lap.

"Thanks, but there's something wrong with it," said Ellen.

Pinky opened the neck of the canvas bag and peered inside. "It looks . . . browner than before," he said.

"I gave it hard-boiled eggs, like you said," said Ellen. "But it didn't eat anything. And it hardly touched the fruit. So I tried cheeseburgers, it loved those."

Rake laughed. "Great present, loverboy," he said.

"Think you should put it back?" asked Ellen.

"Maybe the eggs you got were rotten," said Rake. "I hope you didn't buy them from that Santiago Market." He had stopped welding. He stepped over to Ellen and Oscar caught his first clear shot of Rake. Oscar glanced at the hand holding the welding torch. Below the wrist, spiraling around the right arm, glowed a red dragon tattoo.

9

RUNNING THE MAZE

Rake was the skateboarder from yesterday's accident.

"That Market has lousy food," Rake said to Ellen.

Oscar stepped out from behind the drill press and said, "There's nothing wrong with our food!"

The three students were startled. "What are you doing here?" shouted Rake.

Lily popped her head up from under the table. "You're killing that poor skink," said Lily. "You should know how to take care of an animal before you go and steal it."

"Get outta here," said Pinky.

"And cheeseburgers are bad for it," said Lily. "It makes them angry."

"You're making *me* angry," said Rake.

Lily ignored him. "How did you get into that building?" she asked. "I thought the Bio Lab was locked."

"It wasn't locked once Cruz went in there," said

Rake. "She had to go pick up her papers during her office hours, right?"

So, Miss Cruz unlocked the Biology Building and walked into her office, then Pinky rode up to the auditorium to hide out and wait, and then Lily and her mom entered a few minutes later. While Pinky waited upstairs, he saw the skink and decided it would make a cool present for his girlfriend.

"Who made the bike?" asked Lily.

"I did," said Ellen. "It's an art-and-technology project. But I didn't know they were going to use it to save Rake's butt."

Max stood up next to Lily. "We're calling the police," he said.

Rake's dark eyes were glued to Oscar. "You're the punk on the scooter," he said. "The kid who cheated my buddy out of his ice."

Oscar took a few steps backward.

"What are you snooping around here for?" Rake said. "If you kids don't get out of here there's gonna be trouble. Big trouble."

"Careful, Rake," said Ellen.

"It's my grade," said Rake. "My school year's at stake."

Rake moved steadily toward Oscar. Lily took a deep breath, then scurried over and grabbed the canvas bag from Pinky's lap.

"AAAAHHHHHHHH!"

Rake yelled and dropped to his knees.

"Run!" yelled Max to his friends. He had picked up the weird bike's seat, lying on the floor as it waited to join the sculpture, and lobbed it at Rake's legs. But Rake's yell startled the large skink inside the canvas bag. The bag jerked free of Lily's hands and fell onto the floor, releasing the angry lizard.

"Look out!" cried Ellen.

Pinky jumped backwards off his stool and crashed into the sculpture.

The bike sculpture wobbled. "Oh no," moaned Rake.

"I told you," said Lily. "No cheeseburgers!"

The three-foot lizard scurried in figure-eights across the floor. Its muscular tail beat against the cement like an angry whip. Finally, it shot toward the sculpture, roped one of the handlebars with its tail, and yanked itself off the ground. The sculpture swayed. Rake ran over to catch it, as Lily sprinted toward the door and followed Max and Oscar out into the hall. The three spies jumped onto their waiting scooters and kicked off.

A crash of metal and plastic and lizard rumbled behind them.

"Which way?" yelled Lily. The aluminum walls reflected their scooters like a thousand funhouse mirrors.

"Down here," Max pointed. The hall led to another hallway.

"This is like a maze," said Oscar.

"I think we went down a curvy hall next," said Max.

"We'll be trapped here forever," said Lily.

BANG! The metal doors to the workshop flew open and Rake shot into the hall on his skateboard. "You kids get back here!" he yelled. "I'm not going to hurt you. I just want to talk."

"Yeah, right," muttered Max.

Rake kicked his way toward them on his board.

Lily turned to Oscar. "You're the Ice Boy," she said. "Get us out of here."

Oscar knew he had a terrific sense of direction, but the reflecting walls were distracting him. Their wavy reflections made each wall look the same. Oscar tried a new tactic; he gripped the Fireball's handlebars and lowered his head. He kept his eyes on the floor instead of following the shining, curving walls. It was the same way he had memorized the maze of University buildings. Keeping his head down and following the footpaths and sidewalks and bike trails of the students.

"Faster," said Max. "He's gaining on us!"

Lily pushed and propelled her scooter as never before. The sweat ran down her forehead and stung her eyes.

By glancing into the curving walls ahead of them, she saw the reflected figure of Rake on his skateboard trailing close behind.

Sometimes Max was directly behind Oscar, sometimes Lily. But neither of them could go as fast as the Ice Boy. They couldn't even if they wanted to. He was their only guide back to the outer moat of the pregnant disco-ball Art Center.

"Stop!" shouted Rake. "Let's talk."

Max and Lily were too tired to shout anything back to Rake. They were concentrating all their energy into keeping their scooters racing forward. Keeping out of Rake's reach.

They slid into a sharp zigzag hallway. Rake veered close to the aluminum walls, pushing himself along with his long arms, using the walls to help build up speed.

It's not fair, thought Lily. His legs are longer.

The zig-zag hall led to a straight hall with a downward-sloping floor. The straight hall led to a curving hall. Oscar saw the bronze metal doors ahead of them.

"Just a little farther," he urged his friends.

Max lowered his head. Lily's mouth became a thin grim line. The skateboard rolled closer and closer.

Even if we reach the doors ahead of Rake, thought Lily, there's still the long moat to climb.

Oscar was twenty feet from the door

"Get back here, you punks!" snarled Rake.

Oscar gave a powerful kick against the floor, a final burst of power, when he felt his handlebars lurch. The front wheel that Ernesto had fixed pulled loose from its makeshift pin.

POP!

The wheel broke free and went spinning into the wall.

Oscar sailed off the deck of his scooter. The momentum carried him a good four feet closer to the doors. He never let go of the handlebars. He landed on his sneakers and kept running. With a crash, he pushed the right-hand door and leaned against it, holding it open for Lily and Max.

The Hurricane and the Stingray zoomed out of the doorway, into the sunlight.

Lily glanced up the long ramp and her heart sank. Her lungs were on fire. Max leaned against the wall, unsteady on his legs, his face as pale as his blond hair. Oscar's Fireball had only one wheel left.

Three more seconds and Rake's skateboard would clear the doorway. The spies would not be able to outrace him once he entered the moat.

Oscar slammed the door shut. He still gripped the handlebars of his crippled scooter. The bronze doors of the Art Center each had a metal loop for a handle, like the handles of a refrigerator. Oscar quickly shoved the Fireball's handlebars through the two loops, bracing them shut.

Rake shoved against them from the other side, prying them open several inches.

"That won't hold, you stupid brat!" laughed Rake.

The Fireball's handlebars began to slowly bend.

"How about this?" asked Max. He slipped his Hurricane's handlebars beside those of Oscar's. Lily joined them and shoved hers alongside the other two.

"Triple strength," she shouted.

The doors were secure against the raging Rake inside. He shouted and beat against the bronze doors, but the three sets of handlebars would not budge.

"I think now would be a good time to go and apologize to Pat," said Max.

"And tell him we got a big skink for him," said Lily.

"He needs to bring a cage for it," added Oscar.

"I was talking about Rake," said Lily.

"So was I," said Oscar, with a grin.

READ THE

FINNEGAN ZWAKE

MYSTERIES BY MICHAEL DAHL

THE HORIZONTAL MAN

Thirteen-year-old Finnegan Zwake is staying with
his Uncle Stoppard and life is fairly normal—until
the day Finn discovers a dead body in the
basement. It's in the storage area where Finn's
parents left behind gold treasure from their last
archaeological expedition. And missing from the
storage space is a magnificent Mayan gold figure,
the Horiztonal Man....

THE WORM TUNNEL

Finnegan is off to an archeological dig in sunny
Agualar, land of the giant cacti, jungles, and
dinosaurs. Dead ones, that is. While Finn and his
uncle are searching for treasure, the crew is digging
up very valuable dinosaur eggs. But digging too
deeply can stir up trouble, not to mention a murder,
or two, or three....

THE RUBY RAVEN

Finnegan's uncle is invited to be a finalist in an
international mystery writer's award competition.
That means exotic Saharan travel for Finn and
Uncle Stoppard. The winner will receive $1,000,000
and The Ruby Raven, a figurine of a dark, carved
bird, with the real ruby gems as eyes. All of the
writers are eager to win this coveted award, in fact
some are *dying* to possess it....

Available from Archway Paperbacks
Published by Pocket Books

2133-01